playing **war**

KATHY BECKWITH · ILLUSTRATED BY LEA LYON

TILBURY HOUSE PUBLISHERS · GARDINER · MAINE

"Too hot for basketball," Luke said. "Let's do something else."

They moved to the shade under the willow tree while they decided what to do next.

"Do you have any more water balloons?" Danny asked.

"Nope," Luke said. "I wish we did."

"We could play video games," Sameer suggested with a quick smile.

"No. My mom said we have to play outside."

"I know!" said Jeff. "Let's play war!"

Luke stood up. "Good idea!"

"What about riding bikes?" asked Jen.

"No," Jeff replied. "War's the best! We haven't played it for a while."

"Yeah," Luke added. "We can hide and ambush. Jen, you know you're good at throwing those grenades!"

Jen smiled.

Luke grabbed a stick and scraped a long line in the dirt. On one side of the line he made a big S. On the other side he drew an E.

"First we have to divide into teams—Soldiers and Enemies."

He took off his baseball cap and carefully put it on the middle of the line. The other kids watched.

Jen leaned over and explained the rules to Sameer. "Everybody finds something to put in the hat. Then we dump it all out on the line and see who plays on the Soldier side and who plays on the Enemy side. It's how we start the game. Watch—Luke will put his dog tag in the hat. He always does that!"

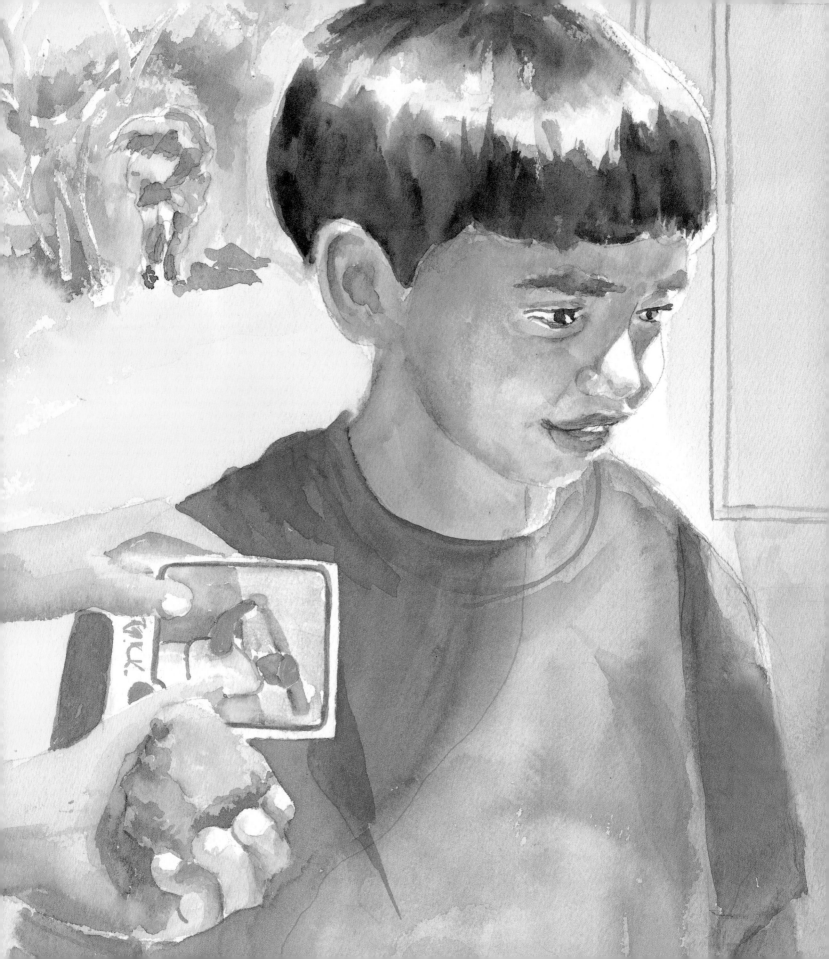

"What's a dog tag?" Sameer asked. He had come from another country to live with his aunt and uncle. Sameer had learned basketball quickly, but he didn't seem to know how to play war.

Luke lifted a shiny metal tag from around his neck and held it out for Sameer to see. "This is a dog tag. It was my uncle's. He was in a real war once, and when he got back he gave it to me. Soldiers wear them all the time. They're really important."

Sameer rubbed the shiny tag with his fingers. "I don't have one of these," he said.

"It doesn't matter," Luke explained. "No one else does. You can put anything you want in the hat. See, Jen's using a rock and Danny is using a baseball card."

Sameer reached into his pocket and pulled out a wooden top. "Can I use this?" he asked.

"What is it?" asked Danny.

"It's a top." Sameer grinned. "Maybe you don't have these here?"

He reached into his pocket for a string. "We had them at home." In an instant the top was whirling at their feet. Sameer popped it up into the air, caught it still spinning, and dropped it into Luke's hat.

"Nice!" said Luke.

Luke turned the hat over with a flick of his wrist and announced,
"The Soldiers are Danny, Jen, and Jeff, and the Enemies are me and Sameer."
Before the others had even moved, Luke was running down the hill.
He shouted, "Enemies to the pine grove. Soldiers stay here."

"Come on, Sameer. You're with me."

Jen yelled back, "No fair starting the war until we're ready!"

   "How do we get ready for a war?" Sameer asked when they reached the trees.

   "Pick up sticks for guns, and pine cones to use for grenades and bombs. And we have to make a plan of attack," Luke answered.

   Within a few minutes Luke's hat was full of pine cones. Sameer had just one in his hand.

   "Only one?" Luke questioned.

   "That's enough," Sameer said.

   "For you, maybe. Not me! I'm going to blow their heads off!"

Sameer handed his pine cone to Luke.
"I just remembered I have to go home early today," he said.
And he left Luke standing in the woods.
"Hey, wait up," Luke called after him. "I can't be the only Enemy.
That's too many against one."

But Sameer was gone.

When the kids gathered the next morning, Luke's plan was ready. He had collected pine cones in the woods behind his house. They were hidden in piles around the yard.

Luke couldn't wait to get started. "I wish they had a war for kids," he said. "A real one. We'd beat anybody—big time."

"They do," Sameer said softly.
"What!" Luke challenged. "Where?"

"At home," Sameer answered. He picked up the basketball and dribbled it to the basket. His shot went in.

"Do you mean where you used to live?" Luke asked.

"Yes, my real home, before I came to live with Uncle Mustafa." He made another basket.

"I was in it," Sameer added. This time the ball bounced off the rim.

"You were in what?" Jeff asked.

"A war."

"No way! You haven't told us anything about that!" Luke said. "A real war? Did they let kids be soldiers? Did you have an M-16?"

Sameer dropped the ball and sat down next to Jen. Even though the kids had played together often this summer, they didn't know much about Sameer's life before he came to live in their neighborhood.

"I don't like to talk about it," he said, taking a breath. "I wasn't a soldier. Nobody in my family was. But we got in the war anyway, when they blew up our house."

"Who blew up your house?" Jeff asked.

"We don't know. Both sides were doing so much shooting." Sameer reached into his pocket, but it didn't seem like he was thinking about the top he pulled out. He started winding a string around it.

"My father, my mother, and my little brother were in the house and they all died. I was at school when it happened. That's why I'm alive and came to live with Uncle Mustafa."

"But why did they hurt your family, Sameer?" Jen whispered.

"It was a mistake. They didn't mean to blow us up. Uncle Mustafa said the shells were supposed to hit somewhere else."

Everybody watched Sameer with big eyes. No one knew what to say. Sameer was talking about something his friends could hardly imagine.

"That's an awful mistake," said Luke, finally.

Sameer nodded. "I wish it never happened."

Hearing Sameer's story made Luke feel like crying. For a moment he just stared at the top in Sameer's hand and thought. Then he stood up and walked over to the line in the dirt, and with his foot carefully erased the letter S and the letter E.

"Aren't we going to play, Luke?" Danny asked.
"Yeah," he answered as he put his arm around Sameer. "Basketball."

Then he looked at his friends and said, "Too hot for war."

TILBURY HOUSE, PUBLISHERS
2 Mechanic Street
Gardiner, Maine 04345
800–582–1899 • www.tilburyhouse.com

First hardcover printing: July 2005 • 10 9 8 7 6 5 4 3 2 1
First paperback printing:

Dedications
To Noor Jasim and all children. —KB
For all the families, no matter what side, who have lost someone to war. And to Erica. —LL

Acknowledgements
Thanks to my cast of characters Farah (Jen), Jeffery (Sameer), Matthew (Luke), Mickey
(Danny), and Vincent (Jeff). I couldn't have illustrated this story without you. And a special
thanks to Freddy the Golden Retriever. Lea

Library of Congress Cataloging-in-Publication Data
Beckwith, Kathy.
  Playing war / by Kathy Beckwith ; illustrated by Lea Lyon.
      p. cm.
  Summary: Dan, Jen, Jeff, and Luke enjoy dividing into soldiers and enemies to play war,
but when Sameer, a new boy in the neighborhood, tells of losing his family in a real war,
they feel differently about the game.
  ISBN 0-88448-267-7 (hardcover : alk. paper)
  [1. Play—Fiction. 2. Games—Fiction. 3. War—Fiction.] I. Lyon, Lea, 1945- ill. II. Title.
PZ7.B381797Pl 2005
[E]--dc22
                                        2004030025

Designed by Geraldine Millham, Westport, Massachusetts.
Editing and production by Audrey Maynard, Barbara Diamond, and Jennifer Bunting.
Printed and bound by Sung In, South Korea.